Guess Who's Coming for DINNER?

Horace & Glenda Pork-Fowler
DUNFASTIN
GLUTTONS WAY

A Templar Book

First published in the UK in hardback in 2004 by Templar Publishing.
This softback edition first published in 2006 by Templar Publishing,
an imprint of The Templar Company plc,
Pippbrook Mill, London Road, Dorking, Surrey, RH4 1JE, UK
www.templarco.co.uk

First softback edition

ISBN-13: 978-1-84011-638-0
ISBN-10: 1-84011-638-2

Edited by Dug Steer

Printed in Hong Kong

For Mum – John
For Tincknells everywhere – Cathy

DUN
FASTIN

templar publishing

Guess Who's Coming for DINNER?

By John Kelly and Cathy Tincknell

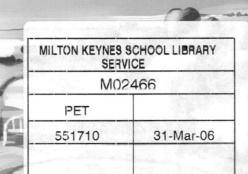

GLUTTONS WAY

Dear Diary,
After an excellent breakfast, a jolly nice letter arrived from Dr Hunter, the new owner of Eatem Hall. He has invited Glenda and me for a weekend of free gourmet food!

It starts tonight, so Glenda has barely seven hours to pack. Should be just enough time for an afternoon snack before we set off!

THE
HOG

Ham Jam

Had a bracing drive up to Eatem Hall, though Glenda was
slightly spooked by the old road through the woods.
She was convinced there were strange noises
out there. Silly old bird!

It was my tummy rumbling!

I must say it was a bit of a disappointing welcome,
what with the door being wide open, and no lights,
staff or food anywhere to be seen.

We were about to turn tail for home
when Glenda spotted a note
on the hallway table.

It was addressed to
Horace and Glenda Pork-Fowler.

My Dear Guests,

Welcome to my home, Eatem Hall.

Due to pressures of business, I am unable to join you tonight, but I have designed this house to offer a fully-automated dining experience. Your every dietary whim can be satisfied by the push of a button or the flick of a switch.

I am delighted to offer you the chance to play a part in the finest dining experience in culinary history, and I will meat you personally in the bandstand on Sunday morning for a final, mouthwatering surprise. An opportunity such as this can only occur once in any lifetime. So, until then – eat, drink and be merry!

Your very special fiend,
Dr A. Hunter F.R.S.W.

Seems like a splendid chap,
after all, even if he can't spell for toffee.

Hunter really is a bit of a brain-box.
He laid on a marvellous spread with his
jolly clever robot thingumabobs. Odd style
of decor, though. Glenda not at all impressed,
but I thought the portrait over the fireplace
was rather good. Especially the way the eyes
seem to follow you round the room.

Proper art, that!

This morning, had a long breakfast and found a splendid picnic hamper waiting for us in the hall! Spent the morning in the grounds, located the bandstand and a poster advertising a feast here on Sunday. Shame we'll miss it — we'll have departed by then.

Rest of the day passed in a blur of wonderful non-stop food.
We did a bit of exercise, and managed to work up a
very respectable appetite for our evening meal.

Still no contact with Hunter, though. Maybe he's a bit of a recluse.

Only closed my eyes for a few seconds while Glenda applied her lotions and whatnot, but when I opened them again, the old girl was snoring contentedly beside me. My stomach however was far from content and was grumbling. Thought I'd pop downstairs for a tiny snackette.

Bit of a long hike to the kitchen. You'd think a clever chap
like Hunter would've put in a lift or something. There are far too
many locked doors in this house, so I was pretty ravenous
by the time I found the kitchen.

Odd, no power in the kitchen, so no robot helpers. Had to fend for myself. Hunter is obviously an extremely keen cook, though. Capital chap keeps a very well-stocked fridge.

Went back to bed eventually,
with a few midnight treats for Glenda!

Today – Sunday – after a leisurely final breakfast we made our way to the bandstand. I have to say it was very poorly constructed and swayed most alarmingly as we climbed.

There was a loud crack as we both
squeezed inside, and since Hunter was nowhere
to be seen, we thought we really ought to leave before
we broke anything else.

Searched for Hunter, but couldn't find him, so decided to set off.
Hoping to get home in time for a late lunch.

As we left, a coach full of guests was arriving for the pie-feast. Dr Hunter must have been too busy making arrangements to give us our surprise.

WOLFELLAS

Never mind.

Shame we never got to say goodbye to Hunter. And "thank you", of course! I wonder what sort of pie they're having?